Leggings Revolt

Monique Polak

Orca currents

ORCA BOOK PUBLISHERS

Library and Archives Canada Cataloguing in Publication

Polak, Monique, author
Leggings revolt / Monique Polak.
(Orca currents)

Issued in print and electronic formats.
ISBN 978-1-4598-1189-8 (paperback).—ISBN 978-1-4598-1190-4 (pdf).—
ISBN 978-1-4598-1191-1 (epub)

I. Title. II. Series: Orca currents

PS8631.O43L44 2016   jc813'.6   C2015-904524-x
C2015-904525-8

First published in the United States, 2016
Library of Congress Control Number: 2015946397

Summary: In this high-interest novel for young readers, Eric and his friends learn
about gender equality when they attend a new high school with a strict dress code.

*Orca Book Publishers is dedicated to preserving the environment and has
printed this book on Forest Stewardship Council® certified paper.*

Orca Book Publishers gratefully acknowledges the support for its
publishing programs provided by the following agencies: the Government
of Canada through the Canada Book Fund and the Canada Council
for the Arts, and the Province of British Columbia through
the BC Arts Council and the Book Publishing Tax Credit.

Cover photography by Getty Images

ORCA BOOK PUBLISHERS
www.orcabook.com

Printed and bound in Canada.

19 18 17 16 • 4 3 2 1

For Carolyn Pye,
librarian extraordinaire.

Chapter One

The first thing I notice when we walk into Lajoie High School is the smell. It's a mix of citrus and vanilla, with a hint of—what is that smell? Fresh laundry. It's definitely fresh laundry. If a guy could get drunk off smells, I'd be out cold on the floor.

Rory punches my arm. "I think we're gonna like it here. A lot," he says.

At first I think Rory has noticed the smell too. But then I realize he is eyeing a tall girl with wavy blond hair.

At the top of the stairs is an oil painting of a woman with a serious face and dark hair pulled back in a bun. Next to her is a poster with a floor map of the school.

Phil studies the map. "The gym is that way," he says, pointing left.

From kindergarten through grade six, Rory, Phil and I went to O'Donovan Academy, an all-boys school. The corridors there smelled of armpits and unwashed gym socks.

"Good morning, gentlemen." It is Mr. Germinato, the principal. We met him at the open house last year.

"Good morning, sir," the three of us say at the same time.

Germinato smiles without showing his teeth. He is standing outside his office.

Because the door is half-open, I notice a wall full of baseball caps.

I have heard of people who collect rare stamps and coins. But a baseball-cap collection? That's a new one.

"That's quite a collection of baseball caps you've got in there," I say.

Germinato swallows his smile. "I don't collect baseball caps," he says. "I confiscate them."

"I, uh, I see," I tell him. "Well, have a nice day…sir."

The three of us make a sharp left, and I nearly crash into the most gorgeous girl I have ever seen. She has pale skin and shiny black hair, and she smells like grapefruit, only sweeter. She is walking with another girl, a redhead with freckles over her nose and cheeks. Their arms are looped together.

I mean to say, *Excuse me*, but what comes out is, "Wow!"

The two girls sail past us, giggling. Rory and I whip our heads around for another look.

The two girls spin around. They must have known we were checking them out.

I feel my cheeks heat up.

"Eric? You're Eric, aren't you?" the gorgeous girl asks.

I look left, then right. She must be talking to some other Eric. One who is taller and smoother with girls than I am. And yet, there is something familiar about her voice. Something angelic.

Rory answers for me. "Yeah, his name's Eric." Then he puffs out his chest. Rory started weight lifting over the summer, and he is always looking for opportunities to show off his pecs. "I'm Rory, and this is Phil. What are your na—"

But the girls turn away before Rory can finish his sentence. They have joined up with another pair of girls, and they are all hugging and making squealing sounds.

"How do you know her?" Rory asks me.

"I, uh, I'm not sure."

Rory sighs. "How could you forget a girl who looks like that?"

"There's more to life than girls," Phil tells him.

"Yeah, like what?" Rory asks.

I can't think of anything else myself, but Phil can. "There's education," he says. "Friendship. Artistic endeavors."

Rory rolls his eyes. "I've got one friend who can't remember a gorgeous girl. And another one who uses words like *artistic endeavors*. I hate to break it to you losers, but I may need to widen my social circle."

When Rory says the word *circle*, it comes to me.

When I was in third grade, my mom was concerned I wasn't reading at the right level. So she signed me up for Reading Circle at the neighborhood library. At first I put up a fight, but then I got into it. Not only because of the books, which were cool, but because of the other kids in the circle. One was this girl named Daisy. She and her family had just moved to Montreal from China. Daisy loved to draw. And there was something angelic about her voice.

That gorgeous girl with the pale skin and shiny black hair?

It's got to be Daisy.

Chapter Two

"Seventh-graders at the front!" a woman in track pants calls out as we file into the gym.

The three of us find spots on the floor. The eighth-graders are behind us. One of them, a guy with pale, wispy dandelion hair, taps my shoulder and passes me a Handi Wipe.

When I shrug, Dandelion-Hair whispers, "For fighting off germs. I figured since you guys are up front…"

"I get it," I whisper back, trying not to laugh. "Germinato."

Germinato walks into the gym, and everyone stops talking, even the teachers. The only sound in the room is the whir of the ceiling fans. Germinato tightens the knot on his tie and tests the microphone by tapping on it. Staticky noise fills the air.

"Good morning," Germinato says, clearing his throat. "I'd like to begin by welcoming those of you who are new to Lajoie High School." Is it my imagination, or does he eyeball the three of us? "And to those of you who were here last year, welcome back. I'm going to use this morning's assembly to review the school rules."

The rules are the usual blah-blah. No running except for in the gym. Report to the office if you are late for class. If you are late three times, you can expect a detention. Cell phones used during class will be confiscated. Swearing and rude remarks are strictly prohibited.

I scan the gym for Daisy. She must be sitting somewhere up front too.

Someone at the back of the gym coughs. Then someone else sneezes. "Gesundheit," a voice says.

After two more rounds of coughing and sneezing, I realize it's a joke. I lean closer to Phil. "Germinato," I whisper. "Get it?"

If Germinato gets it, he does not let on. He talks right over the coughing and sneezing.

"As you know, there are no uniforms at Lajoie High School." When Germinato mentions uniforms, I scratch my neck. It's as if I can still feel the starched white collar of the shirt that was part of the uniform at O'Donovan.

"But we do have a dress code. And we adhere to it. Strictly." Germinato smiles as he says the word *strictly*. "This morning I noticed that many of you were dressed in ways that violate the Lajoie High School dress code. Since this is the first week of school, the dress code will not be enforced. However, it will take effect as of next Monday."

Germinato rattles off the regulations. "No baseball caps. No tops with spaghetti straps. No visible bra straps. No visible midriffs. No shorts or skirts shorter than the reach of your fingertips." Germinato steps away from the microphone to demonstrate. He extends his arms, tapping the spot on his thighs where his fingertips end. "Basically, nothing that could *distract*"—he emphasizes the word—"your fellow students at Lajoie High School. Because the focus at Lajoie is neither fashion nor fun. It is"—he pauses—"education."

A hand flies up into the air at the other side of the gym. "Can I ask a question, sir?" It's the redhead who was walking with Daisy. Daisy is sitting next to her. I think she's got a sketchpad on her lap.

Germinato shakes his head. "Not right now. I'll leave time for questions at the end of my presentation. What I want to discuss next is our Student Life Committee. We need one representative from every grade. If you are interested in serving on this committee, you will have to fill out a form and write an essay outlining your platform. My assistant, Miss Aubin, can provide more details."

A tall thin woman standing at the side of the gym waves one hand in the air. That must be Miss Aubin.

"Elections for the Student Life Committee will be held at the end of next week," Germinato says. "You may now proceed to your homerooms."

"What about the question period?" the redhead calls out.

Germinato checks his watch. "Unfortunately, we're nearly out of time. But I will take one question."

The redhead's arm is raised, but Germinato looks around the gym to see if anyone else has a question.

Nobody does, so he turns back to Daisy's friend. "All right, Rowena," he says in a tired voice. "What's your question?"

Rowena stands up. "Sir," she says, "the dress-code regulations you mentioned are directed mostly at girls. Except for the baseball caps, which are unisex."

"Do you have a question, Rowena?" he asks, drumming his fingers on the podium.

"I do have a question," Rowena says. "Are there any dress-code rules specifically for the male students at Lajoie?"

Germinato tightens his tie again. If he keeps that up, the guy is going to choke. He clears his throat. I think he is buying time while he tries to come up with an answer.

"Well, are there?" Rowena asks.

Germinato sighs into the microphone. "No," he says. "There are not." He checks his watch. "I'm afraid we're out of time. Your homeroom assignments are posted outside the gym."

As we pile out of the gym, Dandelion-Hair is walking in front of us. He nudges the guy next to him, and I hear him ask, "So who do you think is the hottest girl at Lajoie?"

The guy turns to the left, then to the right, scanning the gym. "It's hard to decide," he says. "This place is full of hot girls."

"I know how you feel." I blurt the words out without meaning to.

Dandelion-Hair turns to face me. "Let me guess," he says. "You're a new arrival from an all-boys school."

I nod. "Yup. O'Donovan."

"Well, then," he says, "you've just died and gone to heaven."

Chapter Three

I am waiting for Rory and Phil outside
the Villa Maria metro station when I get
a whiff of grapefruit. Daisy is walking
up to me. She is wearing an orange top
and pink shorts. I cannot help noticing
that one of her bra straps is showing.

"Hey, Eric," she says.

"Daisy." My voice squeaks when I
say her name. She can probably tell that

I have no experience talking to girls. "It's been years. How ya doing? D'you still like to draw?"

"I'm okay. And yeah, I still draw— fashion sketches mostly. But hey, I'm kind of in a hurry. I need to use the washroom." She pats her backpack. I blush because I think she is telling me she is having *a female issue*. Why else would she need to use the bathroom at a metro station? Everyone knows they are the grossest bathrooms in the city.

"Well, good luck." As soon as the words are out of my mouth, I realize how dorky I sound.

But Daisy does not seem to notice. "If you're still here when I'm done, we could walk to school together."

"That would be amaz—I mean, sure."

Rory and Phil show up. I am about to explain that I want to wait for Daisy when she taps my elbow. It takes me a few seconds to figure out why she looks different, but then I realize she has put on makeup. Her lips are bright red, and her eyes are rimmed in black pencil.

So that's what she was doing in the bathroom.

I notice Daisy noticing me noticing her. "My parents," she says. She shrugs, and I spot the second bra strap. "They think I'm too young for makeup. They're almost as bad as the Germinator."

Rory slaps his thigh. "Germinator," he says. "That's a good one."

As we walk down Monkland Avenue, Rory inserts himself next to Daisy. This bugs me. Daisy is my friend. If it were not for me, Rory would never be talking to her.

"Hey, Daisy!" Rowena is heading toward us. "Cool outfit! I never would've thought of putting pink and orange together, but it works."

"You know me and bright colors," Daisy tells Rowena. "I can't resist them."

Then she introduces me to Rowena, and I introduce Rory and Phil.

"What you said yesterday at the assembly was cool," Phil tells Rowena. "I never thought about it before, but dress codes are kind of sexist."

You would think Rowena would like that comment, but she rolls her eyes. "Kind of sexist?" she says. "Dress codes are not *kind of* sexist. They're *totally* sexist. Is anyone telling *you* not to show your cleavage?"

Phil takes a step away from Rowena, as if she is a snake spitting venom. "This may be a technicality," he says, "but guys don't *have* cleavage."

Rory wants in on the conversation. "Unless you mean butt cleavage." He laughs at his own joke. "What I don't understand," he says to Rowena, "is that you're dressed kind of"—he pauses to find the right word—"plain."

Rory has a point. Rowena may be against the dress code, but Germinato would not have a problem with her clothes. She is wearing a white T-shirt and a pair of loose-fitting jeans.

Rowena rolls her eyes at him too. "You're missing the point. It shouldn't matter *how* a girl dresses. It's her choice. It's a guy's problem if he gets distracted by a girl's midriff or her cleavage."

When she says that, I can't help sneaking a peek at Daisy's midriff. "It *is* kind of distracting…" I didn't mean to say the words out loud, but it's too late to take them back.

Rowena shakes her head, but Daisy bursts into laughter, which makes me laugh too. "Relax," Daisy tells Rowena. "Eric and I have known each other forever. It's not like he sees me as some kind of object."

"She's right." I hope I sound convincing. And because I feel Rowena watching me, I add, "Girls are not objects."

"If you really mean that," Rowena says, "you know what you should do?"

"What?"

I can tell from the creases in Rowena's forehead that she is hatching a plan.

"You should run for the Student Life Committee."

Chapter Four

Which is how I end up in front of Miss Aubin's desk. When I tell her my name, she closes her eyes. I get the feeling she is sorting through the files in her brain. She opens her eyes. "Eric Myles. You're one of the boys from O'Donovan, aren't you?"

"Yes, ma'am." Grown-up women like being called *ma'am*.

Miss Aubin removes her glasses and peers up at me. "So how are you liking Marie Gérin-Lajoie High School so far?"

"I'm liking it. Quite a bit, actually. It's a lot bigger than O'Donovan. Plus it's got girls." I should probably not have mentioned the girls.

The corners of Miss Aubin's thin lips rise a little. "Girls," she says. "Of course. I hope they're not causing you to be too *distracted*." If she was not the Germinator's assistant, I'd guess she was making a joke.

"Uh, well, a little." Something in the way Miss Aubin watches my face when I speak makes me want to be honest with her.

"That's perfectly normal," she says. "You'll need some time to adjust to being in a coed school. Now, how I can help you today, Eric?"

"I'm thinking about applying for the Student Life Committee. The Germ—"

I catch myself. Is it my imagination, or does Miss Aubin nearly smile again? "I mean, Mr. Germinato said we should come to you for further information."

Now Miss Aubin smiles for real. "It's wonderful that you want to get involved, Eric." She hands me two sheets of paper. "The first is a questionnaire. The second outlines what is expected in the essay. Basically, you should explain your motivation." Miss Aubin rests her chin on her hand. "Why do you want to run for the Student Life Committee?"

At first I think Miss Aubin is only explaining how to write the essay, but then I realize she really wants to know.

"To tell you the truth, I was talking with a couple of my friends." Is it too soon, I wonder, to call Daisy and Rowena my friends? "About how I'm opposed to the way the dress code works. And one of them suggested I run for the Student Life Committee—"

Miss Aubin does not let me finish my sentence. She tilts her head to the side to check that the door to the Germinator's office is closed. He must be in there trying on baseball caps. "Eric, if I may give you a word of advice, don't mention the dress code." Then she lowers her voice. "Mr. Germinato reads all of the essays. You could mention recycling though. He likes that."

"Great. Thanks for the advice," I say. "Also, what did you call the school earlier? I thought everyone calls it Lajoie High School or just Lajoie."

Miss Aubin walks me out to the hallway. She stops in front of the portrait of the woman with her hair in a bun. "That's Marie Gérin-Lajoie. The school was named after her," she says. I notice a gold plaque at the bottom of the frame. It says *Marie Gérin-Lajoie, 1867–1945*. The way Miss Aubin is gazing at the painting, you would think Marie was her grandmother. "She was a fascinating woman," Miss Aubin says, and I'm not sure if she is talking to herself or to me. "Ahead of her time."

It's not until I am on my way to class that I realize I could have made Miss Aubin's day by asking her what made Marie Gérin-Lajoie so fascinating to her.

As I walk into the classroom, something else occurs to me. Miss Aubin's bra strap was showing.

Chapter Five

So far, Life Sciences is my favorite class. The teacher, Mr. Farrell, is cool, and there are three times as many girls as guys in the class. Rory noticed that on the first day. "I'd say our odds are pretty good," he said. He wasn't talking about blackjack.

Daisy and Rowena are sitting at the back. Rory has already grabbed the desk next to Daisy's. Because I spent most of recess with Miss Aubin, I have to take the only empty desk in the middle of the front row.

We are doing a unit on baboons. We have already learned that there are five species of baboons that live in Africa and southwestern Arabia. They have long muzzles and sharp teeth, and their predators include crocodiles, lions and sometimes humans.

"Today you'll be taking notes on the baboon life cycle," Mr. Farrell explains. He tells us how in the wild, baboons live to be about thirty. In captivity, they can live up to forty-five years.

"Yeah, but who wants to live in captivity?" Rory calls out.

Another teacher might get ticked off at someone calling out, but not Mr. Farrell. He steps away from the whiteboard and asks whether anyone else wants to contribute to the discussion.

Rowena's hand shoots up. "We all live in captivity," she says with a sigh. "I don't mean to depress you guys, but we're trapped in this building until the bell goes at 3:15 PM."

Mr. Farrell chuckles. "Four fifteen, in my case. I'm supervising in the detention room."

Now Rory's hand shoots up. "Should we write that down in our notes?" he asks. Even Mr. Farrell chuckles at that as he turns back to the whiteboard.

"Between the ages of four and five, female baboons reach menarche." Mr. Farrell is looking around the class. I can tell he wants to know if we are familiar with the word. I think I know what it means, but because it's embarrassing, I pretend to study my notes.

"*Menarche*," Mr. Farrell says, "refers to menstruation. Like human females, female baboons get a monthly period."

There's some giggling, and someone whispers something about baboon-sized sanitary napkins. "There's no need to be embarrassed," Mr. Farrell says. "Menstruation is perfectly natural. There would not be baboons—or humans, for that matter—without it.

"Male baboons take a little longer to mature than the females do," Mr. Farrell continues. "Another parallel to the human life cycle—and something I am sure some of you have noticed."

The girl next to me nods.

Mr. Farrell writes the words *reproductive signaling* on the whiteboard. It turns out that to signal her fertility, the female baboon wags (Mr. Farrell does not say *wags*—he says *presents*) her swollen rump in front of the male baboon's face.

Phil raises his hand. "Excuse me, sir, but is this a joke?"

"This is not a joke," Mr. Farrell answers. "It's Life Sciences."

Mr. Farrell goes to the computer on his desk. Thirty seconds later, we are looking at the hot-pink, swollen rump of a female baboon. Mr. Farrell has projected the image on the whiteboard. It could be the grossest thing I've ever seen.

"Are you saying male baboons think that's sexy?" Rory asks.

Mr. Farrell nods. "I suppose they do."

Some of the girls giggle. Other students squirm in their chairs. The girl next to me covers her eyes.

Mr. Farrell stands perfectly still at the front of the room, without saying anything. I think he is giving us a moment to settle down.

"Earlier in today's class, Rowena drew an interesting parallel between the experience of baboons and our own human experience. She pointed out that, like baboons who live in captivity, we too are sometimes restricted in our actions.

"Now, if I may draw your attention back to the screen, can you think of any parallels between the female baboon's reproductive signaling and our own society?"

I think I know where Mr. Farrell is going. I raise my hand. "Are you talking about how girls dress, sir?"

"I'm not talking about how girls dress, Eric. You are," Mr. Farrell answers.

"Well, uh, I guess some girls dress in a way that is, I mean, could be…meant to attract guys," I say.

Mr. Farrell looks at the rest of the class. "Do any of you want to respond to what Eric just said?"

I should not be surprised that Rowena has a response. "Why do you automatically assume that how girls dress is about guys? Why can't a girl's clothes be a form of self-expression? I have a friend who wants to be a fashion designer. Her clothing choices are part of her identity."

I know she means Daisy. "Uh, I guess it could be that too," I say, trying to dig myself out of the hole I did not realize I was digging.

Mr. Farrell saves me. "Eric and Rowena, you've both raised valid points. I think the lesson for today is that Life Sciences is not only a class you take to pass seventh grade. The life sciences affect us all. At every moment."

Chapter Six

Rory was not kidding about wanting to widen his social circle.

When Phil and I get to the cafeteria, we hear Rory's loud laugh from the other end of the room. He is huddled at a table with his new pals. There is Martie, who trains at Rory's gym, and Theo. Rory shares a locker with Theo.

"Should we go over there?" Phil sounds nervous.

"Why not?" I say, though I can think of a few reasons.

"Hey," Rory says as Phil and I sit down. Rory goes back to his conversation with Theo and Martie without introducing us. It's hard to tell what they are talking about. I hear them mention numbers—eight, seven, seven point five. Rory is good at math, but I would not have pegged Theo or Martie as the kind of guys who discuss math over tuna sandwiches. This goes to show how wrong it is to make assumptions about people.

"Are you guys in accelerated math?" I ask Theo and Martie.

Theo grunts. Martie looks at me like I am from Saturn. "What are you talking about?" he asks.

"Well, I figured…since you're discussing numbers…"

Rory guffaws. "That's a good one, little buddy!" I like that Rory has called me *buddy* in front of the other guys, but I wish he had left out the *little* part.

The blonde girl we saw on the first day of school walks past our table. She is wearing a black T-shirt with red cut-off pants and carrying a tray with salad. Alfalfa must be her favorite food.

"Seven-point-five," Theo says.

Rory scratches his head. "Eight."

Then Martie adds, "Seven. Definitely seven. Not round enough."

"What's not round en—" But before the words are out of my mouth, I figure out what the three of them are discussing. Not math. They are rating girls' butts on a scale from one to ten.

My mind flashes on the photo of the female baboon's swollen rump. I blink to make the image go away.

Another girl walks by. This one is about a foot shorter than the blond.

Martie uses the back of his hand to wipe tuna off the side of his mouth. "Seven. Too round."

Theo sighs as if to say rating girls' butts takes a lot of effort. "Eight," he says.

Rory high-fives Theo. "Hey, that's what I was going to say." Rory punches my arm. "So what do you say, Eric?" Then he looks past me at Phil. "What about you?"

Phil tenses up next to me. I have never heard Phil make the kind of comment about a girl that Rory and his pals are making. So I nearly fall off my chair when Phil says, "Seven," and then adds, "I agree with Martie. Too round."

Now all four guys look at me. I consider saying this is a dumb game and asking if they realize they are objectifying girls. But I can already hear them laughing at that.

"Uh, seven-point-five," I say.

Martie leans across the table toward Phil and me. "You two should come to the gym sometime."

I spot Daisy and Rowena in line, buying lunch. I lower my head so they won't see me. If they come to sit over here, the guys will rate their butts. And I will have to do it too.

Rory sees them. And then he does something I really wish he would not. He waves them over.

"You friends with that girl Daisy?" Theo asks Rory. Theo sounds impressed.

"Actually, she's my friend," I say.

Daisy and Rowena stop at a nearby table to talk to some other girls, giving us a perfect view of their butts.

"Ten. Eight-point-five," Rory says.

"Ten. Eight," Theo calls out.

"Not so loud," I tell him, but it is too late.

Rowena turns to face us. She looks like she just tasted sour milk. "Are you guys doing what I think you're doing?" Her voice is so shrill that kids from other tables are turning around to see what is happening.

Rowena grabs Daisy's arm and whispers something in her ear.

I can tell from the way Daisy's eyes are flashing that she is angry too. The worst part is that she seems to be especially angry with *me*. "I thought you were better than that," she hisses at me before she storms off with Rowena.

Chapter Seven

"Where are you going?" Theo asks when I get up from the table.

"I'm going to talk to Daisy and Rowena," I tell him. "To apologize."

"Apologize for what?" Rory asks, and then he guffaws, which makes Theo and Martie crack up too.

"Do you want me to go with you?" Phil offers. I think he is as eager as

I am to get away from Rory and his pals.

"Sure. But I should do the talking."

At first Daisy and Rowena ignore us. But after I apologize twice to Daisy's back, she turns around and says, "Do you promise never to do that again—ever?"

I cross my hands over my heart. "I promise."

"Me too," Phil chimes in.

Rowena only wants to know one thing. "Are you going to run for Student Life Committee?" she asks me.

"I already got the application from Miss Aubin."

Rowena eyes me. I think she is deciding whether I can be trusted. "If you get elected, do you promise to fight the dress code?"

I cross my hands over my heart again. "I promise."

I did not need to work so hard on my application letter for the Student Life Committee. Since I'm the only seventh-grader who applied, there is not going to be an election for our grade.

I am in the library, catching up on homework, when Germinato makes the announcement on the PA system. "The first Student Life Committee meeting is noon on Wednesday in the board-room. There will be a catered lunch," Germinato's voice booms. "Thank you and have a good day."

Rowena is working in the next cubby. "Way to go, Eric!" she says, reaching over to clap my shoulder. "Just don't forget your promise."

The librarian turns to look at me. I am expecting her to shush us. But she smiles and mouths the word *Congratulations*.

"Hey, Rowena." I whisper because I want to stay on the librarian's good side. "Can I ask you something?"

Rowena rocks on the back legs of her chair. "Ask away," she whispers back.

"How come *you* didn't run for Student Life Committee? I mean, you've got strong opinions and all."

"That's exactly why I didn't run. Besides, it would have been a confl—" Rowena stops herself.

"A conflict?" I ask.

"Something like that," she mutters. "If you don't mind, I need to get back to my math homework."

We are studying in our cubbies when Daisy comes up behind us. "Hey, you two," she says. Then she taps my shoulder. "Congratulations on getting elected to the Student Life Committee."

"I wasn't exactly elec—" It is hard to get the words out, because Daisy looks so amazing. Because her hair is in a ponytail, I notice how high her cheekbones are. She is wearing a short

turquoise dress. I see both bra straps—
and quite a lot of leg.

I think Daisy has noticed my reaction, because she says, "It's a new dress.
I mean, an old dress. I got it at a garage
sale. It's from the sixties. Turquoise was
really popular back then."

"I like it." It's hard not to stare at
Daisy. I try looking at the floor instead.
The carpet is beige and worn on the
spots where kids have pulled back
their chairs. My eyes travel to Daisy's
feet. She is wearing fuchsia flip-flops.
Her toenails are the same shade of
turquoise as her dress.

"You'd better hope the Germinator
doesn't see you now that the dress code
is in effect," Rowena tells Daisy. "From
what I've heard, none of the teachers
will turn you in, but the Germinator's
obsessed with that stupid dress code."

"Don't worry," Daisy says. "I plan to
stay out of his way."

It is just plain bad luck that when we leave the library Germinato is standing by the turnstile. I put my arms on my hips in an attempt to block his view of Daisy. "Good afternoon, sir." I keep my voice as casual as I can.

"Eric," Germinato says. For a minute, I think my plan has worked. But then his expression changes. He has spotted Daisy.

"Young lady." Germinato's voice sounds louder than it did over the PA system.

"Yes, Mr. Germinato?" Daisy does not sound nervous.

"It appears that you are in flagrant violation of the Lajoie High School dress code. What do you have to say for yourself?"

"Flagrant?" Daisy says. "I don't know that word." For a moment, my mind flashes on the Daisy I first met in Reading Circle, the shy newcomer who was more interested than any of us in learning new words.

"It means 'total' or 'utter,'" Germinato says.

Rowena has come to stand next to Daisy. "It's extremely hot outside, sir," she says. "And inside too, since this school has no air-conditioning. Daisy is dressed to keep cool. Also, she bought her dress at a garage sale, so it's a form of recycling."

Germinato glares at Rowena. "It doesn't matter where her dress came from. What matters is that she's not abiding by the Lajoie High School dress code. Young lady"—he turns back to Daisy—"consider this a warning. Next time, and I certainly hope there won't be a next time, there will be consequences. Serious consequences."

Chapter Eight

The Student Life Committee meets every other Wednesday at lunch. Germinato left out who was catering the lunch. It's the same company that runs the school cafeteria, which isn't saying much.

A platter with sandwiches sits on the middle of the boardroom table. I grab an egg-salad on brown bread. The bread is so soggy my thumb goes right through it.

I am the youngest member of the Student Life Committee. The president is a girl from eleventh grade named Vicky. The vice-president is a guy from grade ten named Ivan. There is also a treasurer plus five other members at large, like me.

Someone knocks on the board-room door. It's Germinato. Miss Aubin is behind him. "I won't be long," Germinato says. "I want to have a few words with you. As those of you who served on the committee last year know, Miss Aubin will act as secretary. Which means she'll attend all your meetings."

Miss Aubin gives us a tight-lipped smile. She sits down at the end of the table and opens her laptop. Something tells me she is skipping lunch.

"I want to congratulate all of you on being elected or"—Germinato looks at me—"acclaimed to the Student Life Committee. As I'm sure you realize, being part of such an important committee is an excellent addition to your résumés. Which is why I know I can count on your full cooperation." Germinato smiles at Vicky and Ivan, and they beam back at him.

"This afternoon," Germinato continues, "I need every member of this committee to help with an initiative that is close to my heart." At first I think the initiative will have something to do with recycling, but then he says, "The enforcement of our school's dress code."

I look at the other students seated around the table. A couple of them are nodding. A girl is doodling on the back of her notebook. The rest have blank looks on their faces. So I raise my hand.

"Have you got a question?" Germinato sounds surprised.

"More of a comment, sir. You see…I was wondering if maybe we could discuss the dress code and the way it targets…"

Miss Aubin shoots me a look over the top of her computer.

Vicky flicks a spot of lint from her navy-blue sweater. Then she looks up at Germinato. "What is it you need us to do for you, sir?" she asks.

It's as if Germinato did not even hear my comment. "I need you to go to every gym class this afternoon to ensure that every student is wearing regulation-length shorts." Germinato extends his hands by the sides of his legs the way he did at the opening assembly. For a second he reminds me of a wooden soldier.

Miss Aubin catches Germinato's eye. "Sir, it is the beginning of the school year, and this could put them in an awkward position with their classmates."

She pauses, as if she wants to give Germinato time to consider her words. "I could do it, sir."

Germinato waves his hand in the air. "Last time I checked, Miss Aubin, I was the principal of this school, not you."

Miss Aubin's lower lip quivers as she types something on her laptop.

"We'll do it, sir," Vicky says.

"Absolutely," Ivan adds.

"But—" I begin.

Vicky cuts me off. "Eric, we value your participation on the Student Life Committee." She smiles in a way that tells me she does not mean it. "But there's something you need to understand. The newbies on this committee, well, they don't usually say much."

Ivan nods. "It's not that we don't *want* you to participate, Eric. You need some time to learn how things work around here."

"I think Eric is a quick study," Miss Aubin says, without looking up from her computer.

Before Germinato leaves, he hands around a list of all the gym classes for the afternoon. The first group are grade sevens.

I get a knot in my stomach as I remember the promise I made Rowena.

"Do I have to do it?" I ask Vicky when the meeting is over.

"Only if you want to stay on the Student Life Committee," she says.

"Maybe I should resign…" I mutter.

Ivan pats my shoulder. "Didn't you hear what Mr. Germinato said about having this on your résumé?"

I thought Miss Aubin would go back to her office, but it looks like she is coming to the gym too. "Eric," she says, in a half-whisper as we walk together, "sometimes the best way to effect change is from the inside."

Chapter Nine

The first person I see when I walk into the gym is Rowena. It would be hard to miss her. She is wearing a pair of Bermuda shorts—with pictures of palm trees and convertible cars on them. The best thing about those shorts is they go almost to Rowena's knees.

Maybe this won't be so bad. Maybe all the girls will be wearing regulation length shorts. We may not like the school dress code, but hey, isn't it easier to go along with the rules and not fight over every little thing?

Vicky punches my shoulder. "You got this, Eric?" she asks me.

I take a deep breath. "I got it."

Miss Aubin goes to speak with the gym teacher. They huddle for a moment, then the gym teacher whistles to get the class's attention. "Ladies and gentlemen," she says, "the members of the Student Life Committee are here to verify that your gym clothes meet the dress code."

"You mean whether the *girls'* clothes meet the dress code!" Rowena calls out.

The gym teacher does not respond to Rowena's comment. Instead, she asks Vicky and Ivan to be as quick as possible. "I wouldn't want this… this inspection…to interfere with our broomball game," she says.

"It shouldn't take long," Vicky assures her. Vicky turns to the class. "If you could all line up along the back wall, with your hands extended by your sides, Eric will check that your shorts are regulation length." It is obvious from Vicky's tone and the way she puts her hands on her hips that she likes telling people what to do.

I scan the gym for Daisy, but I don't see her. She must be in another class.

As I am thinking that, the gym doors swing open and Daisy sails in. My heart sinks when I see that she is wearing extremely short shorts.

Daisy looks from the back wall, where her classmates are lined up, to me and the other members of the Student Life Committee, then over to the wall again. I can tell she has figured out what is going on. For a second, I wonder if maybe she will try to leave the gym.

Can't she go hide out in the bathroom until the inspection is over?

But Daisy does not make a run for it. Instead, she gives me this giant smile that makes my knees wobble. Then she walks over to the back wall and stands by Rowena. I try looking down at the gym floor, but my eyes are refusing to take orders from my brain—because next thing I know, I am sneaking a peek at Daisy's legs, which are still slightly tanned from summer. I swear, if I was a painter, I'd paint them.

Next to Rowena's shorts, Daisy's look even shorter.

"Eric." It's Vicky. I get the feeling she has already called my name, but I might have been, well, distracted. "Eric." Vicky sounds annoyed. "Let's get this over with. Now." She lifts her chin toward the back of the gym.

"It's not fair! Look how short your fingers are! Mine are almost twice as long!" I hear a girl complain to the girl standing next to her.

I look back at Vicky. She must have heard the girl's comment too. It's a valid point. If a student has long fingers, her shorts need to be longer than if she were a short-fingered person. Maybe Vicky will say we need to review the rules. But I catch her eye, and she lifts her chin again. She is telling me to get on with it.

My heart is thumping. If only there were some way for me to get out of this situation. But there isn't. Not if I want to stay on the Student Life Committee. Then I hear Miss Aubin's words in my head. *Sometimes the best way to effect change is to work from the inside.* But how does that help me now? A guy who is trapped can't effect change.

I move to the end of the line, as far away as I can get from Rowena and Daisy.

The first two students are guys in baggy khaki shorts that go to their knees. They lower their arms, and I make a point of checking where their fingers reach even though I know their shorts are regulation length.

The second guy salutes me—which makes some of the other kids laugh. I feel my ears getting hot.

Next in line is the girl who sits next to me in Life Sciences. I take a quick look at her shorts. They are burgundy and made of sweatshirt material, but they are not as long as Rowena's. My breathing quickens. This is going to be close. I really hope she has short fingers. She extends her arms. Am I the only one who sees that she has folded her fingers so that her knuckles line up with the bottom of her shorts? I nod as I pass her. She nods back—at least, I think she does. The nod was so small and quick I might have imagined it.

The next couple of girls are wearing jeans that are cut off at the knee. None of the guys' shorts are a problem.

Rowena is next. She smirks when I lean down to check where her fingertips end. I know she is remembering the promise I made her.

Some kids have been whispering, but when I get to Daisy, the whispering stops. Everyone is watching us.

I catch Daisy's eye. *I'm sorry*, I say, mouthing the words.

Daisy drops her arms to her sides. She does not bother trying to fold her hands. Her shorts are so short they barely reach her wrists.

I want her to tell me it's okay, that she understands I have no choice about turning her in. But when I look at her again, Daisy just stares at me blankly. As if we never met in Reading Circle or walked to school together.

I force myself to meet Daisy's eyes. "Your shorts, uh, they're not regulation length." My voice cracks on the word *length*. Rowena laughs, and my ears get hot again.

Vicky and Ivan have come to stand next to me.

"You have to report to Mr. Germinato's office," I say. At least this time my voice doesn't crack.

"Now?" Daisy asks.

"Now!" Vicky barks. "Eric, you go with her!"

Chapter Ten

Miss Aubin follows us as far as the library. "I'll see you two downstairs," she says. "And good luck." At first I think she is wishing only Daisy good luck, but when she catches my eye, I realize she means me too.

Daisy walks ahead of me. I try to catch up, but she walks faster. She must be ticked off. I don't blame her.

I take the opportunity to sneak a peek at her legs. Without meaning to, I sigh.

Daisy slows her pace. When she turns around, she looks worried. "Is something wrong?"

"Uh, no, nothing. It's just that…you look really good in those shorts."

"You must like red and blue," Daisy says. To be honest, I hadn't noticed the color of her shorts. I only noticed how good she looks in them.

"Look, Daisy, I'm really sorry about this. It wasn't like I had much of a choice."

"I heard you tell Rowena you were going to take a stand against the dress code," Daisy says, shaking her head.

I hate that I have disappointed her. "I tried," I tell her. "Sort of. Apparently, the seventh-grade member at large doesn't get much say."

Daisy makes a snorting sound. I guess she doesn't find my argument very convincing.

Germinato's office is around the corner.

Daisy bites her lower lip. "I hope he doesn't call my parents," she says.

Germinato is standing in the hallway, near the painting of Marie Gérin-Lajoie. "Good afternoon, sir." I speak quickly, because I want to get this over with. "Vicky asked me to bring Daisy to your office. As you have probably noticed, her shorts aren't regulation length."

Germinato makes *tsk*ing noises as he eyes Daisy. "Young lady, what do you have to say for yourself?"

Daisy throws her shoulders back and looks Germinato squarely in the eye. "I think your dress code is stupid. And sexist."

Germinato's cheek twitches. "That will be enough," he says. "As long as I am the principal of this school, you will abide by my rules. And because this is your second infraction this year, there will be a punishment." Germinato's eyes brighten.

From where I am standing, I can see Daisy fiddling behind her back with her fingers. She is more nervous than she is letting on.

"You're going to change out of those…those clothes—immediately. Pick something out of there." He gestures to the giant lost-and-found bin in the hallway. "Once you're properly attired, you'll knock on my door so I can approve your outfit." With that, Germinato returns to his office.

Now it's Daisy's turn to sigh. She must be relieved Germinato didn't mention anything about contacting her parents.

Since Germinato did not send me back to class, I figure I might as well stick around. I want to support Daisy, but mostly I want to hang out with her.

I help her hoist open the lid of the lost-and-found bin. The smell of mold and mothballs makes us both take a few steps back.

"Let me guess. He's forcing you to wear something from the lost and found." It's Miss Aubin. "There are a few decent things in there," she tells Daisy. "Check the very bottom of the bin."

"Yeah, but what about the odor?" I say.

"I happen to have a steam iron in my drawer," Miss Aubin says. "Pick something," she tells Daisy, "and then I'll give it a quick steam. That should reduce the odor."

Daisy pinches her nose as she sorts through the clothes. "Gross," she says, pulling out oversized gray sweatpants and handing them to me. "Some people have absolutely no fashion sense."

I have never seen anyone sort through clothes so quickly.

"What am I supposed to do with all this stuff?" I ask, but Daisy does not hear me.

"I can't believe anyone would wear this," she says, holding up a pair of jean overalls before she adds them to the pile of discards I'm holding.

I am starting to feel like a human clothes rack.

Miss Aubin supervises from her desk. "Reach all the way down to the bottom," she tells Daisy. "I put some of the better stuff there"—she lowers her voice—"so he wouldn't find it."

Daisy reaches to the bottom of the bin and practically disappears into it. When she speaks, her voice is muffled. "There's just more sweatpants and sweatshirts."

Miss Aubin gets up from her desk. "There were a couple of cute T-shirts that I'd bet you like. Here, let me have a look," she tells Daisy.

But Miss Aubin can't find the T-shirts. "*Someone* must have taken them from the lost and found."

Daisy and I look at each other. We both know that someone must be Germinato.

Daisy grabs a pair of gray sweatpants and a baggy gray T-shirt from the pile of clothing I am holding.

I am still there when she comes out of the bathroom wearing the oversized clothes. "You still look good," I tell her.

Daisy marches past me and over to Germinato's office. She raps on his door. From where I am standing, I make out a hint of a smirk on his face when he sees her. "You'll wear those lost-and-found clothes until school is out this afternoon," he says.

Daisy bows her head for a moment, then looks up. "You can force me to wear these hideous clothes for the rest of the day. But I won't call them *lost-and-found* clothes, Mr. Germinato. They're *shaming* clothes." Then Daisy throws back her shoulders and adds, "And I refuse to be shamed."

Chapter Eleven

Two days later, the temperature plummets. The trees outside are still leafy, but some of the leaves are beginning to turn yellow or red.

The mood at school is different too. We spend longer at our lockers, stuffing hats and mitts into the sleeves of our jackets. The corridor smells like mothballs. Most of us are still wearing runners, but some of the girls are in high boots. It's hard to imagine that soon we'll need winter boots, and the snow will be as high as the schoolyard fence.

The only person wearing shorts today is an eleventh-grade boy with hairy legs. Maybe all that hair acts as insulation.

I am going to miss the warm weather. In a few weeks it will be too cold to play basketball or baseball outside. And I may have to wait till spring to see Daisy's legs and midriff again.

Just as that thought is going through my head, Daisy breezes by. "Did you see Rowena?" she asks me.

I figure the fact that Daisy has spoken to me is a sign I have been forgiven for turning her in to Germinato. "Nope," I tell her.

Daisy takes off her pea jacket and stuffs it in her locker. She is wearing a black top that goes to her waist and black leggings. They give me a perfect view of Daisy's legs.

Maybe I'll be able to handle the cold weather after all.

Rowena shows up next. She is wearing baggy camo pants. I look down the hallway and notice a few other girls in leggings. The rest of the girls are in jeans or sweats. Maybe now that the cold weather is on its way, we can forget the dress code for a while. And the Student Life Committee won't have to do Germinato's dirty work.

"Hey, I haven't seen those leggings before," Rowena says to Daisy. "Are they new?"

"Yeah," Daisy says. "I bought them with my babysitting money. They're made of breathable bamboo—and they're super comfortable." Daisy flexes one leg to demonstrate. "D'you like my new leggings?" she asks me.

"Oh yeah." And because I worry I sounded like some kind of pervert, I add, "They make you look like a gymnast— or a ballerina."

I'm not used to complimenting girls. But I think I'm getting better at it, because Daisy laughs and does a pirouette.

I don't know if it's Daisy's legs or her grapefruity smell or the fact that she is talking to me again, but my math textbook slips out of my hands. When I reach for it, I lose my footing. Next thing I know, I am sprawled on the floor like a bug on its back.

While Daisy and Rowena are helping me up, Germinato comes marching down the hallway. He stops in front of us and shakes his head in disapproval.

"Let me guess!" he says, eyeing Daisy's outfit. "You were distracted!"

I stumble to my feet and wipe some dirt off my sleeve. "N-no, sir, I swear it wasn't that. I dropped my notebook, and I—"

Rowena clears her throat—something about the way she does it reminds me of how Germinato clears his throat before he makes a speech. "I'd like to point out that Daisy's outfit is not in violation of the Lajoie High School dress code—" Rowena pauses before adding the word, "Sir."

"She's right," Daisy says. "My midriff isn't showing, and neither are my bra straps. And my legs are completely covered. Leggings have been a stylish fashion trend since the early 2000s, sir." I am afraid Daisy may do another pirouette. I am grateful she has the good sense not to.

All Germinato says is, "Hmmm," but what he does next worries me—he whips a small notebook and pencil out of his front pocket and jots something down.

I can't tell what he is writing, but I notice he underlines it twice.

Rowena imitates Germinato when he's out of earshot. "*Hmmm.*"

In Life Sciences class, Germinato's voice crackles over the PA system.

Mr. Farrell raises one finger in the air so we will know to pay attention.

"Good morning, students," Germinato says. "I want to let you all know that there has been an addendum to the Lajoie High School dress code. As of tomorrow, leggings are strictly forbidden. Thank you and enjoy the rest of your day."

The girl next to me isn't too happy. "My mom just bought me three new pairs of leggings," she mutters to herself.

Rowena groans. "That's the dumbest thing I ever heard," she calls from the back of the classroom. "A person can't just go around making up rules whenever he wants to."

Mr. Farrell raises his finger in the air again. "That's where you're wrong, Rowena. A person *can* go around making up rules whenever he wants to—if he's the principal."

Chapter Twelve

"Did Rowena put you up to it?" I ask Daisy the next morning at the metro station. She is wearing the same black leggings she got in trouble for wearing yesterday.

"I put myself up to it." Daisy's dark eyes shine. She is more offended now than when I turned her in to Germinato.

"I'm not saying Rowena bosses you around or anything."

Daisy puts her hands on her hips. "It sounded like that's what you were saying."

"It's just that Rowena is a very strong person. She talked me into running for the Student Life Committee. And that didn't exactly work out." I avoid looking at Daisy. "Aren't you worried you'll get in trouble?"

Daisy unbuttons her coat to show me the long grey sweater she is wearing over the leggings. "This tunic top passes the fingers test," she explains.

"I don't know," I say, shaking my head. "He said leggings are strictly forbidden. He didn't mention anything about tunic tops or the fingers test."

Daisy shrugs. "If Germinato thinks leggings are too revealing, he shouldn't object to an outfit that covers our butts and thighs. Rowena says it doesn't make any sen—" Daisy stops herself.

So Rowena *is* behind this!

Which is why, when Rowena meets up with us, I am surprised that *she* is not wearing leggings. She gets prickly when I ask her about it. "The Germinator and I have a complicated relationship," is all she'll say.

When we get to school, Miss Aubin is standing by the painting of Marie Gérin-Lajoie. "Good morning," she says to us. She raises an eyebrow at Daisy's leggings.

"Miss Aubin, can I see you in here for a moment?" Germinato's voice booms from his office.

"I'll be right there, sir." Miss Aubin waves us away with the back of her hand. "Keep out of his way," she whispers to Daisy.

But Germinato must have heard her whispering, because he comes ng out of his office like a bear whose hibernation has been disturbed.

"What's going on out here?" he asks.

The three of us are already rushing down the hall. "Rowena!" Germinato calls after us. "Do you have something to do with this?"

Rowena pretends not to hear him, but her face is flushed.

"Daisy!" Germinato's voice bellows behind us. "Get back here this instant!"

For a split second Daisy freezes. Then she turns around and starts walking back toward Germinato. I hear her take a deep breath.

"You go with her," Rowena hisses.

I could tell Rowena that she's being bossy. But I don't. Instead, I follow Daisy down the hall. I need to hurry, because she is picking up speed.

Germinato has a wild look in his eyes.

"You can't even see my leggings, sir," Daisy says.

Germinato laughs, but it's not a happy laugh. It's a diabolical laugh—the kind you'd expect from a madman, not a school principal. "I certainly can see them!" he says. "Once again you have violated the Lajoie High School dress code. And since this is your third offense, Daisy Fung, I have no choice but to suspend you for three days. Wait here while I phone your parents."

"My parents?" Daisy's voice quivers. "Please don't do that, sir."

Daisy's plea makes Germinato laugh even harder.

I have to do something. Even if it means getting in trouble. "Mr. Germinato. Sir," I say. "You made that rule up yesterday. Isn't that kind of"—I suck in my breath before I say the next word, since I know it will tick him off—"arbitrary?"

I was right about ticking him off.

"*Arbitrary*?" Germinato shouts. "For your information, all rules are arbitrary, young man! Now go to your class this instant, or I'll suspend you too!"

Daisy turns to me. "You should go," she whispers. Her eyes are watery, like she is fighting back tears.

I am sitting by the window in math class when a navy-blue car pulls up in front of the school. A couple gets out, and I know they must be Daisy's parents. They walk quickly into the building without speaking to each other.

I can't concentrate on fractions. I keep checking to see whether the car is still there.

Daisy's parents must be talking to Germinato.

The next time I check, Daisy's parents are walking in single file toward the car. Daisy trails behind them, her shoulders hunched and her head bowed.

Since the temperature dropped, the heat has been on full-blast at school, and the windows are tightly sealed. It feels like I'm watching a pantomime.

Daisy's dad waits at the curb while her mom gets into the passenger seat. Just before Daisy steps into the backseat, she looks back at the school. This time, she is not able to hold back the tears.

Chapter Thirteen

It's day two of Daisy's suspension, and no one has heard from her. Not even Rowena. Daisy has not answered my Facebook messages, and Rowena says Daisy is not answering her phone. Rowena thinks Daisy's parents confiscated her phone and are not letting her use the home computer. "They're crazy strict,"

Rowena says. "They're almost as strict as *my* parents."

"You have strict parents?" Somehow that isn't what I pictured.

Rowena rolls her eyes. "If you don't mind, I'd prefer not to discuss my parents."

"Okay, fine. Do you think we should go over to Daisy's?"

"*We*? There's no way I'm going there. The Fungs hate me. They think I'm a bad influence."

Which is how, that day after school, I end up on Daisy's doorstep, mustering up the courage to ring the doorbell.

When I do, I hear footsteps and then I can feel someone peering at me through the peephole.

"Daisy?" I step a little closer. "Is that you?"

"Who are you—and what do you want?" a woman's voice asks. It must be Daisy's mom.

"Hello, Mrs. Fung," I say. "My name is Eric. You met me and my mom a long time ago at Reading Circle." I figure it's best not to mention Daisy straightaway.

"Reading Circle?"

"Yes, ma'am. At the library."

Mrs. Fung opens the door a crack. "Why are you here?" she asks.

"I came to…uh…see how Daisy is."

"Daisy was suspended from her school." Mrs. Fung's voice drops when she says the word *suspended*.

"I know. That's why I came to see her."

Mrs. Fung looks me up and down, trying to decide whether I am a bad influence like Rowena.

"I'm on the Student Life Committee." That's the only thing I can come up with.

Mrs. Fung opens the door and gestures for me to come in. "Daisy!"

she calls upstairs. "Eric from Student Life Committee is here. You can come downstairs for a few minutes."

Daisy comes downstairs wearing pink flannel penguin pajamas. She has a sketchpad with her.

"Hey, Daisy." I know I'm smiling. Daisy has that effect on me.

I wish Mrs. Fung would go away and give me a chance to talk to Daisy in private, but it is clear that that's not going to happen.

"Have you been sketching?" I ask Daisy.

"Uh-huh." She opens the sketchpad to a drawing of a girl wearing a ruffled dress—with leggings.

"Very nice," I say. Because Mrs. Fung is supervising, I decide not to make a comment about the leggings. "People at school are really upset about what happened to you," I say instead.

Mrs. Fung shakes her head. "Daisy was not following the rules," she says.

Daisy bristles. "I hate when you talk about me as if I'm not standing right here!" she hisses.

"Daisy!" Mrs. Fung says—and Daisy hangs her head.

I turn to Mrs. Fung. "Ma'am," I tell her, "the rule Daisy got in trouble for—well, it doesn't make any sense."

Mrs. Fung raises one finger in the air. "It does not matter whether the rule makes sense. What matters is that it is a rule. My husband and I are starting to think Lajoie High School is not the right place for our Daisy. We think she needs a stricter environment."

"Stricter?" Daisy wails. "You've got to be kidding, Mom."

"Mrs. Fung, I really think—"

But Mrs. Fung is not listening to either of us. "Go upstairs," she tells Daisy. Then she turns back to me.

"You'd better leave now. And it's best if you don't come back."

On my way into school the next morning, the strap on my backpack comes loose. I stop to fix it in front of the painting of Marie Gérin-Lajoie. Miss Aubin is standing there too—gazing into the eyes of her idol.

"Why, Eric," Miss Aubin says when she realizes I'm standing next to her.

"I, uh…didn't mean to interrupt you two." Then, because I realize how weird that sounds, I add, "Not that you were having a conversation or anything…"

Miss Aubin smiles. "In a way we were. I start every workday by taking a moment to communicate—in my own fashion—with Marie Gérin-Lajoie. She is my inspiration."

"If you don't mind my asking—what did she do that was so inspiring?"

"I'm always surprised how few students know about the woman after whom their school is named," Miss Aubin says. "Marie Gérin-Lajoie was one of Quebec's first feminists. In 1922, she led a protest for women's suffrage, which means the right to vote. Did you know, Eric, that Quebec was the very last province in Canada to grant women the right to vote?"

"No, I had no idea."

"And that didn't happen until 1940. It was a long, slow battle, but Marie Gérin-Lajoie never gave up the fight."

Now I look into the eyes of the woman in the portrait too. She does look determined. "What do you think she'd say about the dress code?" I can't resist asking Miss Aubin.

I half expect Miss Aubin to turn to see whether Germinato's door is open, but she doesn't. "She'd say the dress code was ridiculous." Miss Aubin does not even bother lowering her voice.

Once again I find myself feeling like I can confide in Miss Aubin.

"I went to Daisy's house yesterday," I tell her. "The Fungs want to move her to a stricter school. Do you think there's any way to stop them?"

When Miss Aubin answers, I get the feeling she is also speaking to the woman in the portrait. "There is always a way. It's just a matter of finding it."

Chapter Fourteen

"Is it just me—or does it smell like O'Donovan in here?" Phil says when we walk into Rory's gym.

The gym is in the basement of an industrial building. A middle-aged man is lifting hand weights in front of a mirrored wall. Sweat dribbles down his neck.

Rory is spotting some guy on a bench press. The guy grunts as he lifts a giant dumbbell into the air. When he drops the dumbbell into its holder and turns his head to the side, I realize the guy is Theo.

Theo mops the sweat off his brow with the back of his hand. "Hey," he says to Rory, "look who's here."

Martie is doing push-ups at the back of the gym.

Rory shows us where the locker room is so we can change. "Don't look so worried," he tells Phil. "We'll start you with five-pound weights." Then he looks over at me. "Maybe the two-point-fives."

Theo is friendlier than I'd expected. "Don't worry about how much weight you're lifting," he says. "What counts is your form." He demonstrates a set of curls with the five-pound dumb-bells. "You want to exhale while you're lifting. Like this…"

Martie joins us, adjusting his shoulders to give us a better view of his biceps.

I catch my reflection in the mirror. I can't help noticing how scrawny I look. I wonder how many push-ups it would take for me to look like Martie.

"Speaking of form," Martie says, "how's your friend Daisy doing?" Martie licks his lips, which makes Rory and Theo burst into laughter.

I guess they expect Phil and me to laugh along with them, but I'm not in a laughing mood. Don't they see they're being jerks?

Phil answers Martie. "Eric went to Daisy's house after school yesterday. Her parents want to transfer her out of Lajoie." Maybe Phil is nervous. He can't stop babbling. "Eric said her mom thinks she needs a stricter environment. I bet you anything they'll send her to Queen of the Mountain. The principal there makes the Germinator look like Mother Teresa…"

Martie flexes his forearm. "We can't let a girl that hot be transferred out. We gave her butt a perfect sco—"

That's the moment I decide I've had enough. "Don't talk about Daisy like that!" I snap.

Even Phil looks surprised—and slightly worried. "Martie was kidding, weren't you, Martie?" Phil says.

"Yeah sure, I was kidding," Martie says, though I don't believe him. "I didn't mean to tease you about your girlfriend, little guy."

Now I know Martie is looking for a fight. Why else would he call me *little guy*? If this gets physical, I don't stand a chance. But even if Martie beats the crap out of me, I'm glad I'm standing up to him. I've had enough.

I think of how Germinato and the other students on the Student Life Committee ignored me and how I'd had to turn Daisy in. I did not stand up either of those times, but I am standing up now. Even if it's gonna hurt.

"Daisy isn't my girlfriend," I tell Martie. "And you know what else she isn't?" The strength in my own voice takes me by surprise and gives me the courage to go on. "She isn't an object. And that's what you guys are doing. You're treating them like objects. Girls weren't made for us to ogle. They're people. And in case you haven't noticed, Daisy is a really interesting person."

Theo wags his finger in the air. "I'm a little confused," he says. "Weren't you rating girls' butts in the cafeteria too?"

I feel my ears heating up. "I did," I say. "But I didn't feel good about it. And I apologized to Daisy and Rowena afterward."

Theo rolls his eyes. "Poor baby didn't feel good about it." Then he sticks his thumb in his mouth and wails like a baby.

"I didn't feel good about it either," Phil says softly. Then, in a louder voice, he adds, "Eric's right. We need to stop objectifying girls." Phil looks into Theo's eyes. "D'you have a sister?"

"So what if I do?" Theo asks.

"A younger sister?" Phil asks.

"She's in fifth grade."

"How would you feel if you heard guys talking about her the way we've been talking about girls?"

Theo doesn't answer right away.

"You wouldn't like it, would you?" Phil says.

"Okay, okay, we're getting it," Martie says. "What do we have to do to show you guys we see your point?"

That's when the lightbulb goes off inside my head. "You can join the Leggings Revolt," I tell him. "It'll be a way for us to help Daisy and every other girl at Lajoie. And our participating will

95

show we don't believe in treating girls like objects."

"Did you say *Leggings Revolt*?" Phil asks.

"That's exactly what I said."

Rory and Theo are laughing again, but they stop when Martie extends his palm in front of them. "Leggings Revolt," Martie says. "I like the sound of that. We're in, right, guys?"

"I guess," Rory says.

Theo nods. "We're in."

After our workout, Theo wants to stop at the store for a carton of milk.

"Milk?" I put my thumb in my mouth the way Theo did before. "Now who's being a baby?"

As we walk toward the store, Theo tells Phil and me that drinking milk helps build lean body mass. Rory and Martie are discussing the Leggings Revolt.

I hold the door for someone leaving the store with a brown bag.

"Hey, did I hear someone say *Leggings Revolt*?" the person asks. That bossy voice can only belong to one person—Rowena.

The others have recognized her too. "You heard right," Rory tells her. "Eric came up with the name Leggings Revolt. All we need now is a plan of action."

Rowena sets her brown bag down on the sidewalk. Something tells me she is about to boss us around. "We should start a petition," she says.

Chapter Fifteen

By the next morning, Rowena has
come up with the wording for the petition. *We, the undersigned, object to
the Lajoie High School dress code on
the grounds that it is sexist and targets
female students. We believe the new
leggings rule is totally arbitrary and
therefore unfair. We insist the leggings
rule be abolished, and we also insist*

the entire dress code be rewritten, with input from every student at the school. Furthermore, we want Daisy Fung's suspension to be struck from her record.

Rowena has made a dozen copies so we can start collecting signatures. She hands me her pen and points to the first blank line on the sheet.

"Shouldn't you be the first to sign?" I ask her. "It was your idea. And you did all the work."

"I'd rather not be the very first one." When I ask why, Rowena folds her arms across her chest and says, "It's complicated."

Collecting signatures is more fun than I expect. Because there are still fifteen minutes before homeroom, I start in the hallway, tapping kids' elbows and telling them about the petition. Soon there is a thick crowd of students pressing in on me. Everyone wants to sign.

"Great idea!" a girl says as she adds her name. "It's about time we stood up to the Germinator."

"Do you really think this'll work?" Dandelion-Hair asks as he scribbles his signature.

"It's worth a try," I tell him.

The girl from Life Sciences class tugs on my sleeve. "I can't believe Daisy Fung got a three-day suspension for wearing leggings," she says. "I want to sign." When she signs, I learn her name is Maude.

An older boy claps my back as if we are good friends. "Hey, do you think you could add something about getting our baseball caps back? The Germinator confiscated my Expos cap two years ago. That thing is worth big bucks on eBay."

"You're Eric, aren't you?" another kid asks.

"Sure am," I tell him. For the first time since I started coming to Lajoie

High School, I feel like I belong. Had I known political activism could make a guy popular, I'd have stood up sooner! Even older students who usually treat seventh-graders as if we're air are treating me with respect.

My sheet already has thirty-five signatures. It's a good thing Rowena printed lines on both sides.

I tap the elbow of the person next to me. "Would you like to sign this petition to make changes to the school dress code? I've got a pen if you nee—"

The elbow I tapped belongs to Ivan from the Student Life Committee. Vicky is with him. They have the same sour expression on their faces.

"What are you thinking, Eric?" Ivan grabs the petition from my hand. "*We, the undersigned*," he begins reading in a high-pitched nasal voice.

"Give him back the petition," the guy who lost his Expos cap tells Ivan.

Ivan holds the petition up in the air for a second, and then he throws it back at me.

The final bell rings. We have three minutes to get to class. The crowd around me disperses as quickly as it formed. Only Ivan and Vicky are left. "When Germinato finds out you're involved in this, he'll kick you off the Student Life Committee," Ivan says. "Don't you realize how this will affect your résumé?"

"There's more to life than résumés," I tell Ivan. "And in case you haven't noticed, your Student Life Committee is a joke. All we do is carry out Germinato's orders. Doesn't it bother you that the dress code is sexist?"

Vicky has not said a word, but now she points to the petition. "Let me see that."

"You're not going to tear it up, are you?" I ask her.

"Of course not." Vicky's eyes move across the top of the page. I expect her to scowl or say something sarcastic, but instead she plucks the pen from my fingers and adds her signature to the list.

Ivan shakes his head. "That petition isn't going to do any good."

"How do you know?" Vicky asks him.

"My older brother graduated from Lajoie six years ago. He and his friends put together a petition. They wanted Germinato to let them use the gym one Friday a month for school dances. They were even going to give the money they raised to a homeless shelter."

"What happened with the petition?" I ask Ivan.

"He read it, and then he put it in a folder at the very back of his filing cabinet. He didn't even have the good manners to say he'd think about it," Ivan says.

I look down at the petition. It has forty-six signatures. Phil, Rory, Theo and Martie have been collecting signatures too. But even if we get every student at Lajoie to sign our petition, it may not be enough to get Germinato to rethink the dress code.

It's time for more radical action.

Chapter Sixteen

Am I the only kid who gets his best ideas in the shower?

I am soaping my pits when it comes to me. What if, for one day, every single kid at Lajoie High School wore leggings—even the boys? Germinato couldn't suspend everyone! The more I think about it, the more genius my idea sounds.

I want to run it by Rowena, but I don't see her on my way to school.

Germinato is not at school either. I know because there is no car in the *Reserved for Principal* parking spot. The other clue is that Miss Aubin is humming to herself. She never hums.

Mr. Farrell is wearing a tie. "What's up with the formal wear?" Rory asks him when we walk into Life Sciences.

"I'm filling in for Mr. Germinato today," Mr. Farrell says.

"Did Mr. Germinato get suspended?" Maude asks.

I can tell Mr. Farrell is trying not to smile. "Mr. Germinato needed the day off to deal with some personal issues," is all he says.

Mr. Farrell makes us work in pairs. I partner up with Maude. Mr. Farrell hands each pair a section from a map of the world. We get China. We are supposed to add drawings of the animals that are native to our country. Maude is trying to draw a panda bear. I decide not to point out that the animal she is drawing looks more like a cat than a bear.

Maude is the first one I tell about my plan. "I like it," she says. "A lot. You'll need to go viral—spread the word on Facebook and Twitter. Rowena can help with that."

"Too bad she isn't here today," I say.

Maude shakes her head. "I hope everything's okay at her house."

"Maybe she's got the flu."

"Yeah, but her dad's away too." Maude puts her hand over her mouth. "Her dad?"

"Yeah. I probably shouldn't have said anything. You've got to promise not to tell anyone else, okay? The Germinator—he's Rowena's dad."

I slap my thigh. "No way."

"Yes way," Maude says. "Rowena doesn't like people knowing. That's why she uses her mom's last name—Johnston."

No wonder Rowena didn't want to run for the Student Life Committee!

"We used to live around the corner from the Germinatos," Maude says. "My mom thinks Germinato's so strict because of all the problems they've had with Luanne, Rowena's older sister."

"Problems?" I ask.

"She dropped out of college," Maude says as she puts a black spot on the cat-bear's belly. "And now she's pregnant."

"Pregnant?" For the first time, I find myself actually feeling sorry for Germinato. Maybe he thinks that if he had been stricter with Luanne, she might have stayed in school and not gotten pregnant.

Mr. Farrell announces that he needs to leave the classroom for ten minutes.

"I'm counting on you people to continue working together quietly," he tells us before he goes.

Maude gives him time to get to the other end of the hallway. Then she puts two fingers in her mouth and whistles to get the class's attention. "Eric and I need to ask you guys something. Are you ready to join the Leggings Revolt?"

I explain my plan, and every single kid in Life Sciences wants in. Even Rory is willing to come to school in leggings. "I'll borrow a pair from my sister," he says.

"When are we going to do it?" someone else asks.

Maude thinks we should give ourselves a few days to get organized, and to make sure Germinato will be in the building. We settle on Friday. That will give us time to put the word out on social media.

One student is standing guard by the classroom door. "Mr. Farrell's on his way," he tells us.

When Mr. Farrell walks into the classroom, we are working on our illustrated maps. He surveys the room. "It's nice to see such focus in here," he says. "If I didn't know better, I'd think you guys were up to something."

Chapter Seventeen

Word spreads quickly about the Leggings Revolt. I am at my locker when a tenth-grade girl hands me a bag. "For the cause," she says. Inside are three pairs of black leggings. I can use a pair, and I'll give the other two to guys like me, who don't have leggings or a sister to lend them some.

Rowena has set up a Facebook page that already has over two hundred Likes. That's impressive when you consider enrolment at Lajoie is just under six hundred. "You're good buds with Miss Aubin," Rowena tells me. "I bet you could sweet-talk her into giving you a list of email addresses for all the students."

Before, I'd have tried to talk Rowena into doing it, but now that I know Germinato is her dad, I don't bother.

At recess I am back in front of Miss Aubin's desk. Miss Aubin waves me away. "Can you give me five minutes?" she whispers, pointing at her computer screen. I tilt my head, expecting to see words on the screen. Instead, there is a grainy image of Daisy, looking sad, and her mother waving her arms in the background. I have interrupted some kind of online meeting.

I mouth the words *no problem* to Miss Aubin. I consider waving to Daisy, but then decide that would be dumb. Especially since I hope to eavesdrop. I grab a seat about six feet from Miss Aubin's desk. Because I have my World History textbook with me, I flip it open and pretend to study.

Miss Aubin's eyes flit toward me, then away.

"Mrs. Fung, I believe it would be a mistake to transfer Daisy out of Marie Gérin-Lajoie High School," I hear Miss Aubin say.

From where I am sitting, it's hard to make out Mrs. Fung's answer, though I manage to catch the words *rules* and *metro*. The Fungs must know about Daisy's habit of putting on makeup at the metro station.

Now Miss Aubin addresses Daisy. "I'm all for freedom of expression, but I wonder if you've thought about the sort of image you present when you dress in a way that draws attention to your body."

I hear Daisy's answer, which means she must be shouting. "Why should I have to care about my image? Why don't you talk to the boys instead? Get them to stop looking at girls as if we're objects!"

"I see your point, I really do, Daisy," Miss Aubin says. "There's no question that boys' attitudes need to change. But perhaps if you"—Miss Aubin pauses to choose her words—"toned it down, even a little…"

"I only dress to be comfortable!" Daisy insists.

Miss Aubin looks directly into the camera at the top of her computer. "I'm in favor of dressing comfortably. But is it possible that some of your fashion choices might be attracting the wrong kind of attention from the boys?"

Daisy shakes her head. "Whose side are you on anyhow?" she asks Miss Aubin.

"I happen to be on your side, Daisy. I'd just like you to think about the impact of your choices."

"Fine," I hear Daisy say. "I'll think about it." She still sounds angry.

Miss Aubin sighs. "That's good. There's something you should know, Daisy. I'm not the only one who's on your side. The students at Marie Gérin-Lajoie High School want you back, and they want the suspension wiped from your record."

Which makes me wonder if Miss Aubin has seen the petition.

I wait until Miss Aubin calls me over. When I get to her desk, she eyes my textbook. "You weren't really studying World History, were you, Eric?"

"I was, I mean…well, not exactly." Why is it so hard for me to lie to Miss Aubin? "I overheard a bit of your conversation."

"A bit?" Miss Aubin raises her eyebrows.

"Okay, a lot. Thanks for trying to keep Daisy at Lajoie. She's really something, isn't she?"

"I hope you're not referring to her physical appearance," Miss Aubin says.

"Of course not. Though I do like her physical appearance. When I say Daisy is really something, I mean all of her." As the words tumble out, I realize how much I mean them.

"So, Eric, is there something I can help you with today?"

I almost forgot my mission. "We're trying to organize this thing"—I don't want to use the word *revolt*—"to show our support for Daisy. And, well, I was wondering, you wouldn't happen to have a list of all the students' email addresses, would you?"

Miss Aubin grips the edge of her desk. "I could get in all sorts of trouble for sharing that information."

"I guess I shouldn't have asked…"

"All right then, Eric, I'd better get back to work." Miss Aubin looks at her computer and types something on her keyboard. A second later I hear the whir of her printer.

"Okay then, I should get going," I tell her. "Hey, thanks for telling Daisy we're trying to help her."

Miss Aubin's eyes meet mine. "Eric, could you do me a small favor? I left my fruit salad in the staff room. Would you mind my desk and answer the phone? Just say, 'You have reached Marie Gérin-Lajoie High School' and explain that I'll be back in about seven minutes."

"Do you want me to get your fruit salad for you…"

"No," Miss Aubin says. Her tone is firm. "Teachers don't like students in the staff room."

Miss Aubin does not shut down her computer.

You can't blame me for looking at the screen.

My heart beats double-time when I see it is open to a document called *Student Email List*.

I'll be back in about seven minutes.

That gives me just enough time to print the list.

Chapter Eighteen

I don't get much sleep on Thursday night. I am up past midnight, emailing my list of thirty-five students. Rowena, Maude, Phil, Rory, Theo, Martie and Daisy—she is back at school for what her parents call "a trial period"—are each going to contact thirty-five students too. Even Vicky offered to pitch in.

When I finally get to bed, I am too hyper to sleep.

In the morning there's a lineup of teenagers outside the bathroom at the metro. I'm not the only guy who didn't want to leave his house in leggings. I wore jeans over mine, so it doesn't take me long to peel off the jeans and stash them in my backpack.

When I leave the bathroom, I spot Daisy. "Nice legs!" she says to me.

"I hope you're not gonna rate my butt!"

"I would never treat anyone like an object," she says.

We walk to school in a group. I can tell the others feel the way I do, excited and nervous. Excited to be standing up for what we believe, but nervous about Germinato's reaction.

Students are milling around the school's front entrance. Every one of them is wearing leggings! Though we did not specify a color, almost everyone is in black leggings. I do see a few gray pairs, and some with patterns. One girl's leggings have a graffiti design. Germinato is really going to hate those.

I take a deep breath when I see Germinato's car and another as I push open the front door of the school.

But the first thing I see makes me laugh, which relieves some of the tension I'm feeling. A pair of black leggings hangs off the bottom of the painting of Marie Gérin-Lajoie! Who did that?

There is no sign of either Germinato or Miss Aubin.

Some guy in ninth grade taps my shoulder. His leggings are too short, exposing his hairy calves. "What do you want us to do?" The question takes me by surprise. People don't usually come to me for instructions.

"Uh, just do whatever you would normally do," I tell him.

I overhear snippets of conversation around me. "Can you believe how many kids are wearing leggings?" "Where'd you get yours?" "I can't wait to see the Germinator's face!"

I am heading to my locker when Miss Aubin walks out of the staff room. She's wearing leggings! "Good morning, Eric," she says. Then she winks at me.

Now I hear Germinato's voice from the other end of the hallway. "Those leggings violate the Lajoie High School dress code. Report to my office immediately. All five of you, on the double! And you too! And you!"

I swear I feel the blood coursing through my veins, pumping me up. Daisy and Rowena are on the way to their lockers too, their elbows linked. "Maybe you should stay out of his way," I tell Daisy. Then I turn to Rowena. "And you too." I have not told her that I know Germinato is her dad.

"No way!" they say at the same time.

Germinato is standing in the middle of the locker area, waving his arms like some broken robot. His face is red and swollen-looking. "You! Get to my office!" he shouts.

When he sees the three of us, he gets a wild look in his eyes. "What in tarnation is going on here today?" he asks. "It's as if everyone in this entire school is wearing leggings! Rowena! Do you have something to do with this…this disaster?"

As I step forward, the locker area becomes suddenly quiet. I can feel everyone watching me. "Mr. Germinato, sir, everyone in this school *is* wearing leggings. And it's not a disaster. It's the Leggings Revolt."

I want to say more, but Germinato does not let me. "Revolt, my foot!" he shouts. "All of you, to my office now! I am the principal of this school, and you will abide by my rules!"

"Sir," I say, and I hope no one can tell that my legs are shaking, "there isn't room in your office for six hundred students. Maybe you need to rethink the dress code."

Germinato turns his back on all of us and stomps back toward his office. "Should we go to his office like he said?" a girl asks me.

"Like I told him, there won't be room for all of us," I say.

"What if we lined up down the hallway?" Rowena asks.

We hear the crackle of the PA system and then Germinato's voice. "Attention, students and teachers! I am calling an emergency assembly. Everyone to the gym immediately!"

The first thing I notice in the gym is that Miss Aubin is not the only staff or faculty person wearing leggings. Mr. Farrell and half a dozen other teachers are wearing leggings too!

This time no one offers me a Handi Wipe or pretends to cough or sneeze. The gym is a sea of students, all focused on the podium where Germinato is standing. I think we all have the sense that whatever happens, we are making history. From what I can tell, there is only one kid in the gym not wearing leggings—Ivan.

Chapter Nineteen

Germinato grips the podium with both hands. He scowls when his eyes land on the teachers who are wearing leggings.

Because the microphone is on, we all hear him mutter, "Miss Aubin! How could you?"

Every kid in the gym turns to see Miss Aubin walking in. Not only is she wearing leggings, but she is also carrying a cardboard sign with a photo of Marie Gérin-Lajoie on it and a dialogue balloon over her head that reads *Down with the dress code!*

Maude jumps up from her spot on the floor and shouts, "Down with the dress code!" Then, as quickly as kindling catching fire, everyone joins in. Soon the whole gym is chanting, "Down with the dress code! Down with the dress code!"

"Silence! Silence now!" Germinato sputters into the microphone. But the chanting continues.

Germinato taps furiously on the microphone, but that does not work either.

Now Ivan pops up from his spot.

"How come you're not wearing leggings?" someone asks him.

"Because I'm against this revolt!" he shouts back.

Ivan picks his way through the crowd to join Germinato at the microphone.

"Thank you, Ivan," we hear Germinato say. "If you ever need a letter of recommendation, just ask."

Having Ivan at his side reinvigorates Germinato. "Silence! Silence this instant!" he booms into the microphone. Finally, the crowd quiets down.

"I have not failed to notice," Germinato says, "that many of you are wearing leggings, despite the fact that the Lajoie High School dress code prohibits leggings. I am your principal, and I have the right to punish you. All of you"—Germinato looks around the gym, his eyes landing on the students, the teachers and finally on Rowena— "who are in violation of the Lajoie High School dress code…"

I hear whispering behind me, then Daisy saying, "Do it now!"

I'm surprised that for once Daisy is giving Rowena orders. When Rowena stands, her hands are trembling. She is holding a stack of papers. It must be the petition. If she presents the petition to Germinato now, there's no way he can hide it at the back of his filing cabinet.

Rowena walks to the podium, holding the petition to her chest like a shield.

"Go, Rowena!" Rory calls out.

"You rock, Rowena!" Phil adds.

Again that sets the others off, and now there is a chorus of "Rowena!"

Rowena pumps one fist in the air.

"What are you doing, Rowena?" Germinato asks as she approaches.

Rowena steps closer to the microphone, so we all hear her answer. "Da—" She stops herself. "Mr. Germinato, I hereby present you with a petition signed by 549 students at this school. It reads, *We, the undersigned…*"

I don't know who is first to stand up when she has finished reading it to him. Maybe it's Maude, maybe Phil, but now every student is clamoring to his or her feet. And they are all shouting, "Down with the dress code!"

"Fine!" Germinato shouts into the microphone. "I said, *fine!*"

Rowena spins around, her face inches from her dad's. "What do you mean by *fine?*" she asks. Am I the only one who sees the resemblance between the two of them?

Germinato speaks into the microphone. "By *fine*, I mean I will consider your objections to the dress code. And I have decided *not* to impose a punishment on any of you—at least, not today." He smiles as if everything is settled.

When I look over at the benches where the staff is sitting, I realize Miss Aubin is watching me. Is she trying to send me a message?

I shrug my shoulders and raise my palms. It's my way of asking, *What's the message?*

Miss Aubin looks at me—hard.

I know what that means.

She is not going to tell me what to do.

I have to figure things out for myself. It is up to me—and the other students—to affect change. The way Marie Gérin-Lajoie did.

I bring a chair from the side of the room and stand up on it so everyone will see me. I'm not even shaking. I feel like a tree planted firmly in the earth.

"Hey, that's Eric!" someone calls out. "He's the brains behind the Leggings Revolt!"

"Mr. Germinato," I yell, "your offer is not good enough. We don't want you to *consider our objections* to the dress code. We want the leggings rule dropped *now*. And we want your assurance *now* that the dress code will be revised with our input." I turn to look at Daisy. "And we want Daisy Fung's suspension wiped from her record *now*."

Germinato throws his hands up into the air. "Fine!" he says.

And with that, the whole gym erupts into cheering and clapping. The walls vibrate from the noise.

Chapter Twenty

There have been many changes on the Student Life Committee.

Lunch is no longer catered by the school cafeteria. Instead, we get to order in. Today we're having Indian from Monsoon Moon. They make the best samosas and butter chicken in Montreal.

Another change is that everyone has a say—even me, the seventh-grade rep.

Today I am reporting on the dress-code negotiations. "There's been more progress," I tell the others. "Mr. Germinato has agreed to drop the rule prohibiting visible bra straps."

"Did you speak to him about my idea of auctioning off his collection of confiscated baseball caps?" Ivan asks.

I open my binder to the notes I took during my last meeting with Germinato. "He was open to the idea," I say. "As long as the proceeds go to charity."

"*Open to the idea*," Sandy, the ninth-grade rep, says. "I never thought I'd hear those words spoken by Germinato."

I don't tell the others what I know. That Germinato's new attitude may not be the result of the Leggings Revolt. Ever since I told Rowena that I know Germinato is her dad, she has been filling me in about her home life.

It turns out that Germinato and his wife are going to help raise Luanne's baby.

The whole family has been attending weekly counseling sessions. According to Rowena, the therapist has strongly encouraged Germinato to be a better listener to young people.

Miss Aubin raises her hand. She still takes minutes at our meetings, but she has also begun sharing some of her own ideas. "I thought I'd mention that Marie Gérin-Lajoie's birthday is coming up on October 19. I was thinking that perhaps the Student Life Committee might want to mark the occasion."

"We could organize a party in her honor," Vicky says.

"I'd like to see a poster display explaining her role as an advocate for women's rights," Miss Aubin says. "I could talk to one of the history teachers. It could be a class project."

"We should do something with Marie Gérin-Lajoie's portrait," Sandy suggests. "Kids walk by that painting without even looking at it. We need to find a way to make it speak to students."

The word *speak* combined with my memory of the sign Miss Aubin made for the Leggings Revolt gives me an idea. "What if we asked students to come up with dialogue balloons with stuff Marie Gérin-Lajoie might say if she visited our school today?"

Miss Aubin smiles as she includes my idea in the minutes. Then she looks up at me. "I think I know what Marie Gérin-Lajoie would say. She'd say she was proud of each and every one of you. And, *Long live the Leggings Revolt!*"

Acknowledgments

Every book has a story behind it. In winter 2015, I was doing writing workshops with students at St. Thomas High School in Pointe-Claire, Quebec. I happened to show them my ideas notebook and read them my list of book ideas. They liked *Leggings Revolt* best. Then something wonderful happened: they agreed to turn up during several of their lunch hours to share their thoughts about dress codes and, later, to read and critique this story. Many thanks to St. Thomas librarian Carolyn Pye for inviting me to her library and to Quebec's Ministère de l'Éducation du Loisir et du Sport's Culture in the Schools Program, which makes visits like these possible. Thanks to the following St. Thomas students for your enthusiasm and inspiration:

Jeff Chan, Fatma Elgeneidy, Samuel Helguero, Giordano Imola, Matthew Kasovan, Eric Kopersiewich, Kiara Lancing, Magalie Langlois, Maude Larrondeau-Soule, Brianna Losinger-Ross, Madison Moore, William Pugsley, Cynthia Sauvageau, Katharine Scarlat, Owen Stafford, Emma Starr, Lindsay Thomas, Averie Tucker, Marisa Vertolli and Samantha Vissani. And, as always, thanks to the terrific team at Orca, especially my smart and sensitive editor, Melanie Jeffs.

Monique Polak has been known to don leggings. Monique has written numerous books for young people, including five other Orca Currents. Her last Currents novel, *Hate Mail*, won the Quebec Writers' Federation Prize for Children's and Young Adult Literature. Monique lives in Montreal, Quebec. For more information, visit www.moniquepolak.com.